EVERYTHING
CHANGES

For Nicholas, Jenny and Alex

Pantheon Books

EVERYTHING CHANGES

By

MORRIS PHILIPSON

Pictures By

Kelly Oechsli

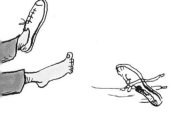

Sometimes the sun shines
Sometimes it rains
Sometimes the wind calls
Sometimes the snow falls

Seeds grow

to roses

to carrots

to trees

From eggs will come

eagles

turtles

and bees

EVERYTHING

LET'S GO METS

all of the time EVERYTHING CHANGES ALL OF THE TIME Everything char
f the time Everything changes all of the time Everything changes all of the t
EVERYTHING CHANGES ALL OF EVERYTHING ing changes all of the t
Everything changes all of the time Everything changes all of the time Everything char
ll of the time Everything changes all of the time Everything changes all of the t
EVERYTHING CHANGES ALL OF THE TIME Everything changes all of the t
Everything changes all of the time Everything changes all of RYTH
HANGES ALL OF THE TIME Everything changes all of the TIME g char
CHANGES thing changes all of the time Everything of the t
verything changes all of the time Ever ALL OF THE of the time Everything char
the time EVERYTHING CHANGES ALL OF THE TIME Everything change

CHANGES ALL OF THE TIME

of the
ERYTHING
erything changes all of the time all of the time
nges all of the time

ything changes all of
of the time Everything chang
Everything changes all of the time
ything changes all of the tim
all of the time EVERYTHI

Dogs were once puppies

Cats little kittens

FROGS

were first

TADPOLES

Hens

little

chickens

EVERYTHING CHANGES ALL OF THE TIME

Cotton's for shirts
and corduroy pants
Silk becomes dresses
to wear at a dance

Wool from a sheep
can make a warm sweater
Gloves, caps and shoes
can be made of soft leather

Everything changes all of the time. Every

anges all of the time

Everything CHANGES ALL OF THE TIME

all of the time
the time Everything changes a

me Everything changes all of the time Ever
all of the time Everything changes

time Everything changes
EVERYTHING CHANGES ALL OF THE TIME
changes all of the time
ALL OF THE T
me Everything
ges all of th
VERYTHIN
changes
of the time

From farm
into village

From village to town

Some things get better
But some things break down

Everything changes
all of the time

Whether they're poor
or have lots of money
Whether they're sour
or
cheerful and funny

Thick, thin
short
or
tall—

People change the most of all

Some who are SAD

can become very HAPPY

Some who are DULL

can become rather
SNAPPY

Children too good
can have fun playing pranks

Others too mean

can learn why to say thanks

Just as a storm
in a rainbow may end

So can a stranger
become your best friend

EVERY TH

EVERYTHING CH

EVERYTHING CHANGES

ALL OF THE TIME

and